The BLUE ROSES

by Linda Boyden

illustrated by Amy Córdova

Lee & Low Books Inc. • New York

LEE & LOW BOOKS Inc., 95 Madison Avenue, New York, NY 10016
leeandlow.com

Manufactured in China by RR Donnelley

Book design by Tania Garcia
Book production by The Kids at Our House

The text is set in Cochin.
The illustrations are rendered in acrylic paint and pencil on gessoed paper.

HC 10 9 8 7 6 5 4 3 2 1
PB 10 9 8 7 6 5
First Edition

Library of Congress Cataloging-in-Publication Data
Boyden, Linda.
    The blue roses / by Linda Boyden ; illustrated by Amy Córdova.— 1st ed.
        p. cm.
    Summary: A Native American girl gardens with her grandfather, who
helps to raise her, and learns about life and loss when he dies, and then speaks
to her from a dream where he is surrounded by blue roses.
    ISBN 978-1-58430-037-3 (HC)   ISBN 978-1-60060-655-7 (PB)
    [1. Grandfathers—Fiction. 2. Gardening—Fiction. 3. Death—Fiction.
4. Indians of North America—Fiction.] I. Córdova, Amy, ill. II. Title.
PZ7.B6943 Bl 2002   [E]—dc21   2001038141

MIX
Paper from
responsible sources
FSC
www.fsc.org   FSC® C144853

To my wondrous family and to the memory of
my grandfathers, John T. Simmons and Edward
Louis Dargis. A special and forever thanks
to J.B. and my editors, Laura and Louise.
—L.B.

To the sacred lives of children. May you grow
and blossom in a safe and loving world.
—A.C.

MOMMA SAID

On the day I was born my grandfather planted a
rosebush under my bedroom window. He dug the
hole deep, threw in a few chunks of dead fish, then
tapped down the soil.

When I was five days old, my grandfather carried
me out to see my rosebush, though I was too little
to see much. He turned my head and I spit up!
Milk dribbled down his hand onto a leaf. My
grandfather laughed and chose my name. Rosalie,
he called me, his little rose.

When I was three, I could not say *grandfather*.
My mouth wouldn't stretch around that great big
word, so I named him Papa. He named me and I
named him, but he never spit up on me!

My mother, Papa, and I lived in a house on a
street with seven other houses. Momma worked
all week long at the fish cannery.

All his life Papa fished on the wide blue sea,
until the sea wind shivered his bones and made
him cough. After I was born he stayed at home
to tend me and his garden.

OUR HOUSE

Papa's garden made our house different from the others. Vegetables grew during the summer—corn and carrots, beans and peas—in rows straight as pencils. Past them, yellow squash and orange pumpkins huddled in mounds like sisters sharing secrets. Flowers bloomed in tiny rainbows along our fence— purple pansies, blue lupines, yellow marigolds, orange nasturtiums. Best of all, the red, red blossoms on my rosebush danced with every breeze.

A Green Thumb the neighbors called Papa.

"The little one too," they said and smiled, but their words made me hide behind Papa's leg. I didn't want our thumbs to turn green. Every day I checked but we were lucky. Our thumbs stayed brown, brown as ever.

Every spring we planted. Papa
hoed the rows. Behind him I dropped
in seeds, round and bumpy or straight
and smooth.

"Tiny promises, seeds," Papa said.
"The promise of a future."

Inside each row Papa placed chunks
of dead fish he carried in an old bucket.
I held my nose against the stink.

Papa laughed. "The bad smell goes
away," he said. "Put in the fish and the
plants will grow strong."

He tickled the back of my neck.
"Rosalie, a garden is the closest place
to heaven on this hard earth."

I listened but secretly hoped heaven
smelled better.

ON MY NINTH BIRTHDAY

Papa planted three new rosebushes around my red bush, two pink and one yellow. "To make a sunset," he said.

He was right. The yellow and pink and red sky did shine in their petals, but I also liked the color of the day sky.

"Papa, could I get a blue rosebush too?"

He thought for a moment. "Roses aren't blue, Rosalie."

I asked him why not, but Papa just shook his head. Then he showed me my other present, my own garden plot!

As Papa watched me hoe my rows, I remembered to stop in the middle each time, to be sure the row ran straight. Papa smiled then, a wide sparkling grin.

"A natural-born gardener, that's my Rosa—"

A coughing spell stopped Papa. He coughed so hard he lost his words. I hurried and helped him to the ground.

For the first time I saw Papa was old, so old that lines zigzagged across his face, and his thin silver braid quivered on his back with each cough.

When Papa caught his breath, he looked in my eyes. "Don't be afraid," he whispered.

I told him I had to be, because he was so old.

Papa laughed. "Old's nothing to fear."

I didn't believe him. I reached to touch one of his wrinkles.

"Wrinkles? They just tell the story of your life."

"What does this one say, Papa?"

He closed his eyes. "One day when I was at sea, the sky turned yellow black. The wind howled, and wave after wave tossed my boat. I clutched the wheel, squeezed my face tight . . ."

"And then?"

Papa leaned on my shoulders to get up. "Then? The storm stopped. I sailed home, and when I looked in the mirror, there it was, my first wrinkle."

Later I stared in the mirror, hoping to find my own story, at least the first line. Instead I found four new freckles.

And in the morning I found two dead pea plants! Right in the middle of the row they drooped, brown leaves curled in empty fists. I threw down my hoe.

"They died!" I cried.

Papa tugged one of my braids. "Everything dies, Rosalie."

"But they were new! They weren't supposed to."

"Everything has its time to die. New or old, it doesn't matter. Pull up the dead ones. Tuck them under the others so they'll help, like the fish."

When I was done, Papa leaned on his hoe. "See how a garden works? Your peas grew, but some died. If you dig them into the soil, something new will come." We stood quiet for a minute. Then he said, "That's what I like about gardens, Rosalie. Nothing ever really leaves."

That night, under my star quilt, I thought about plants, animals, and people having a time to die. I looked out my window.

What about stars? Would they die too? I fell asleep listening to Papa cough, wondering about old people and the stars.

SUMMER TURNED INTO WINTER

Late one night Momma woke me.

"Come say good-bye to Papa," she said gently.

Good-bye? I wondered. I rubbed the sleep from my eyes.

Papa's room glowed with a soft light. He rested quiet, not coughing one bit.

"Shh, Momma," I whispered. "Let's not wake him."

Momma dropped into a chair and hid her face in her hands. Her shoulders shook. I looked and looked at Papa until I figured it out. Papa was dead.

Even though I was almost ten, I climbed onto Momma's lap.

AFTER PAPA DIED

Our house stretched like a huge rubber band around relatives and neighbors. Aunties and uncles, elders and babies filled every room.

The grown-ups laughed and told good stories about Papa. They cried and sang soft songs. The babies fussed and the little cousins gobbled cookies and fry bread. The noises swirled in my head, so I snuck off to the garden.

There I could still smell Papa, and I told my cousin Mitch. He laughed and said I was dumb. Mitch thought he knew everything, but he didn't know how nothing ever really leaves a garden.

After the funeral the days ran down like a music box out of song. I went to school and I walked in the garden. I helped Momma and she helped me, but we missed Papa so much. Sometimes she'd cry. Sometimes I did. Sometimes we cried together.

ONE NIGHT I DREAMED

I was walking through clouds, puffy and white, climbing under them and over, yet never falling through. Higher and higher I climbed until I reached the top.

Then I was standing beside a white fence, looking into a garden of flowers, a whole sea of colors—orange and gold, pink and lavender.

"Rosalie," a voice called. "I knew you'd come."

There was Papa, right in that garden! Straight, not bent. His face was smooth and glowing, not one wrinkle!

"Where are your wrinkles, Papa?"

"Gone, now that my life story's been told."

Then Papa pointed above his head. A trellis of roses curved around him. He pulled a branch lower.

"Blue, Papa! My blue roses!"

He winked and smiled.

I tried to open the gate, to go inside to Papa and the beautiful roses, but he shook his head. "No, Rosalie. You can't come in."

How could that be? We always shared our gardens. I tugged the latch harder but Papa shook his head again. "It won't open for you, my little rose. Not yet."

I started to cry. "But I miss you!"

"And I miss you, Rosalie. We're in different gardens now, that's all. Remember how nothing ever really leaves? You tend the sunset roses and I'll tend the blue ones, and we'll be together."

Papa smiled then, his special smile. It sailed into my heart and made me smile too. In a shimmer he faded like stars to the sunlight.

I awoke in my bed, the sunset roses peeking at the window, the blue roses still in my heart.

THE REST OF
THE YEAR PASSED

I grew two inches and needed new jeans. Momma was promoted at work. I won the Spelling Bee and learned how to multiply fractions.

Missing Papa became familiar, like a cut that heals as a scar. Momma and I still cried, but not every day, not like before.

Planting time came again. I hoed and planted every little seed the way Papa taught me. I even put in the chunks of dead fish.

School ended when the roses bloomed. I tied the longest branches of the sunset roses over my window to grow like the trellis in my dream. I wished on the first star every night for two weeks that they'd turn blue, but they never did.

ONE SUNDAY MORNING

Momma and I ate breakfast at Dipsy's Kitchen—doughnuts thick with chocolate and milk rich with foam. Afterwards we drove to the cemetery to weed around Papa's headstone.

I had planted rosebushes on either side of Papa's stone. Their bright leaves waved hello as we parked. I grabbed my hoe and started toward his grave but stopped. Specks of color flashed from the bushes. Had someone thrown trash on Papa's roses?

I ran fast. Momma too. When we stopped, our eyes stretched wide.

Not trash but tiny roses dotted the bushes, some full, some clenched—hundreds of beautiful blossoms.

All blue! As blue as the sky or the sea or a wish inside a dream. My fingers touched a blue petal and I heard Papa's laugh.